CHECKING THE CENTER

THE WILCOX WOMBATS
BOOK 0.5

DELANCEY STEWART

PROLOGUE - JULIUS RAMON (ZAMBONI DRIVER)

IN HOCKEY, PICKLEBALL COMES FIRST

A truly great hockey coach once told me: "Great opportunities come to those who make the most of small ones."

And when it comes to Rock Stevens, Center for the Wilcox Wombats, I feel like he knows what this means. Even if he probably can't articulate it. The guy is charming, intelligent, and one hell of a center. He's a star for good reason. But he's not necessarily the best talker.

I've been watching him on the ice since he came to the Wombats with something to prove. And while it's not my place to say it, he's made great strides.

Now if someone could just rack down that ego a few notches... he wouldn't just be great. He'd have the potential to be phenomenal.

But first... pickleball.

CHAPTER 1
DREA

THE FUTURE IS DRUNK

"I'm telling you, it's the only answer." Paige Whitehead nodded her head emphatically as she put her beer down a little too hard on the tabletop, liquid sloshing over her hand as she fixed me with a penetrating, if slightly glassy, stare.

"There is no world in which having my future told by a notorious drunk is an answer to anything." I shook my head, glad I'd volunteered to be the designated driver tonight. Paige was listing to one side on her stool.

April righted her sister-in-law with a gentle shove to her shoulder. "Maybe it's not the actual answer, but it can't hurt, can it? And it could be fun." She grinned and wiggled her eyebrows, her pretty blue eyes gleaming.

I sighed and felt my shoulders slump. "Why am I so pathetic?" It was hard to sit here with my friends, feeling so completely alone while I knew each of them would go home to the man of their dreams. They were so stinking happy it was hard not to be jealous. But they were my friends, and even if I was a little envious of the happiness they'd found, mostly, I was glad for them. I just wanted the same thing. Was that too much to ask?

"Drea, she's legendary," Paige said.

"She's known as the drunken psychic of Center County," I reminded Paige. "I'm not sure that's the kind of legend I need right now."

"But everyone says she's legit," April shrugged. "Like I said, can't hurt."

"Okay, let's play it out," I said, taking a second to sip my wine. "We go over to see the drunken psychic. She reads my cards. What in the world can she possibly tell me that will magically solve this for me?"

Both of my friends gave me blank looks over the tabletop.

I waited, and when neither answered, I sighed again and cast my gaze around the interior of Straddler's, the bar we hung out at whenever we had a chance. It wasn't a regular occurrence since both April and Paige had gotten married recently, and we all had busy jobs.

The handsome bartender, Wade, met my eyes and gave me a little salute, so I smiled back at him. "Why couldn't he be single?" I muttered, sending two more sets of eyes toward the bar to stare at Wade.

"He is hot," April agreed.

"So hot," Paige said. "But Ronnie's nice too."

Veronica, or Ronnie, was Wade's fiancée.

"I'm literally the last single person in Singletree." I was feeling sorry for myself, but I couldn't help it.

Paige began to giggle. "Single in Singletree."

"Yes, it's hilarious," I agreed. "You're cut off, by the way."

"Nooo," she complained. But then she straightened her shoulders and nodded. "Yes. That is very responsible. Good."

I thought she'd sobered up in a hurry, but then she melted again into a pile of giggles.

"It's good you don't have to work tomorrow," April told her. "I can only imagine how that would go."

"I'm a doctor," Paige told me with a serious expression, as if I didn't already know this.

"Yep, time to go," I said, standing.

"Okay, but we're seeing the psychic on the way home," April said cheerfully, helping Paige to her feet.

Paige clapped her hands together and cheered at this.

"No, we are not." Seeing a drunken psychic could in no way assist me in relieving myself of singletude. The best bet was to keep on carrying on, living vicariously through my happily coupled-up friends. They were married to two very hot brothers, Callan and Cormac. And I wasn't jealous. I wasn't.

Dammit. I was.

Paige's legs turned to jelly when I said no, and April staggered, trying to hold her up. "Say yes," Paige said.

"Are you seriously throwing a tantrum right now?" I asked her.

"I'll walk if you say yes," she told me, grinning, still doing her best to slump to the ground.

April was struggling to hold up her sister-in-law. "Could you just say yes until we get to the car, at least?"

"We have to really go," Paige insisted, nearly pulling April to the floor.

People were beginning to look our way, and Wade had come around the bar. "You ladies need some help here? Paige, you okay?"

"It's a sit in," Paige told him.

"Well, you're about to sit in a puddle of beer, darlin'," he told her, lifting her back to her feet with a strong arm around the opposite side from April.

"She can walk, but is refusing until she gets what she wants," I told him.

His eyebrows rose, but he didn't ask.

"I learned from the best," Paige told us. "Maddie can stage one hell of a fit to get her way." Maddie was Cormac's youngest daughter, Paige's stepdaughter.

"That's some pretty heavy ammo," Wade said. "What's she demanding?"

"We're going to see the Center County psychic," April told him. "For Drea."

"And Paige doesn't want to?" Paige was still dangling between Wade and April, looking perfectly content as the interest around the bar in our situation faded.

"No, she does want to," I explained. "But I don't."

"I hear she's pretty good," Wade said. "When she's not slurring. And even then, she's usually right. Or she might be. Hard to say when she's unintelligible."

"It's late. She'll probably be drunk," I pointed out.

"I heard she quit drinking, actually," Wade said.

"You are not helping," I told him.

He shrugged. "Let's get this party outside and maybe we can toss a coin or something to get it all settled."

"Yay!" Paige called loudly. "Heads, we go. Tails, Drea goes alone."

"No way," I muttered.

When Paige was finally settled in the back seat of my car, and we'd waved goodbye to Wade, April turned to me over the center console. I could feel her eyes on me, even as I started up the engine in the dark.

"How could it hurt?" she asked. "You want to meet someone. Maybe she can just give you a little nudge in the right direction."

"Maybe Callan has some single soccer friends?" I asked hopefully.

"I've asked him, trust me. He can't think of anyone, at least not around here, though if you're up for long distance, there are some guys coming in for that big pickleball thing."

Paige let out a giggle at the mention of pickleball.

I let out another mighty sigh. This was one of the downfalls of living in one of the most beautiful, but remote, areas of the country. No one knew we were here, and the pickings were slim unless you happened to meet the right guy in high school, or unless he was imported somehow.

"Fine. Let's see the drunken psychic," I said.

"Yay!" Cheered Paige from the back.

CHAPTER 2
ROCK

A SLIGHT CHANCE OF TOMFOOLERY

Going home to Singletree wasn't high on the list of things I was dying to do. Life was good in Virginia. My hockey career was on fire, my teammates were my best friends, and the contract I was about to be offered was going to cement my future with the Wilcox Wombats for the foreseeable future.

"It's an All-Star game," my teammate Sly reminded me as I grumbled about the trip in the locker room after a scrimmage.

"Yeah," I agreed. "And if it was an all-star hockey game, that'd be one thing. But it's not."

"True."

"I mean..." I shook my head. "Pickleball?"

Sly grinned. "Everyone loves pickleball."

"Well, I don't even know how to play. And what the hell is the deal with this craze anyway? I swear to you, my dentist's grandma plays pickleball. Isn't it an old people thing?"

"Is it dark in there?" Sly asked, pulling my confused gaze from the bag I was packing.

"What? In where?"

"Just wondering if it's dark up in your ass where your head has clearly been for the past year. Pickleball is sweeping the nation. I'll have you know, it's the fastest growing sport in the country. Especially among the twenty-five to forty crowd."

I frowned at him. "Have you been reading Wikipedia? Or has some pickleball organization offered you a sponsorship?"

He shrugged. "It's possible a paddle will soon be coming out emblazoned with my name."

I sighed and went back to shoving things into my bag. Somehow I always ended up with more of my personal belongings in the Wombat locker room than in my condo. "Congrats."

"Pickleball is huge. You know LeBron James plays."

"I did not know this," I assured my friend.

"You need some tips?" He leaned in and whispered this as if I might be ashamed to admit I had no idea how to play a game that had been named after a phallic picnic condiment.

"I think I'm good."

"I'm here if you need me."

"Thanks, Sly. I better head out. I guess we have pickleball practice tomorrow morning."

"You'll wanna be fresh." He gave me a knowing wink.

"Right." I wasn't particularly concerned with being fresh for pickleball practice. I was more concerned with sneaking in and out of Singletree without too many people from my past noticing I was there. The town was nuts, and the last thing I needed was any sort of kerfuffle. Because Singletree, Maryland, was the one place in the country where a grown man should worry about things like kerfuffles and shenanigans, and even tomfoolery.

As I slung my duffle over my shoulder and gave Sly a salute, he called after me, "You make the Wombats proud, Rock Stevens!"

"Rock it!" Another of my teammates called from between the lockers a few rows back.

There were a few other hoots and hollers from my teammates, and some more calls to "Rock it" - the standard chant the crowd liked to use whenever I played. It wasn't clever, but I liked it anyway. At least one good thing came from my ridiculous moniker. If you had to be named Rock, you'd better be a hockey player, I figured. Or work in construction, or be part of a motorcycle club. Mom had doomed me with that one, but I'd done the best I could with it.

The drive to Singletree shouldn't have been long, but as I finally crossed the bridge into Maryland, I remembered that it always was. It was partly thanks to Maryland's unique geography, and partly because the town seemed to exist in a vortex of small-town strange that just couldn't be achieved anywhere else, and it took some effort to navigate into that vortex.

It was dark when I pulled up to the duplex I'd once called home. It was a nice-looking, side-by-side double unit owned by my Aunt Nattie, but I'd stayed here most of my adult life. The rent was cheap, and the place was nice. It faced the Patuxent River on one side, and looked out into the woods across the little road on which it sat on the other.

The place was quiet and remote, and perfect for a little winding down.

I parked out front, grabbed my duffle, and put my key into the lock, gratified to step into the place I'd once called home.

I flipped on the lights in the entry, and a jolt of surprise shot through me. Aunt Nattie had evidently decided to redecorate. There were some feminine touches added here and there—a framed picture on the wall of some seaside scene, a couple candles scattered around. It wasn't a lot, and I guessed it added a nice touch.

Whatever. I wasn't here to stay, just to crash for the week.

I dropped my duffle on the living room floor and made my way to the kitchen. I was pretty sure I'd left some beer in the fridge, and that was exactly what I wanted. To drink a beer and flip on the television, take in the last match between our long-time rivals—the Quill Boars—and their neighboring franchise, the Roosters.

There was a lot of random crap stuffed into the fridge, which made me wonder what the hell Aunt Nattie had been doing with my place in the eight months since I'd left it. I still paid rent every month, so I wasn't crazy about her using it for much of anything, but then again, my rent was a fraction of what it should have been, and it was her house.

I pushed aside the abundance of vegetable matter and non-dairy milk choices—how did one get milk from an oat, I wondered—and let out a sigh of relief to find the six pack I remembered leaving still there, standing at the back of the space, waiting patiently for my return.

"Hello, girls," I said, pulling one out.

I'd have to talk to my aunt tomorrow to figure out what she'd been up to and see if I needed to offer her more money each month to keep the place the way I liked it. I didn't come back often—there was little reason to besides my aunt and my cousins, who all had lives of their own. But I liked knowing the place was here, that it was still home.

I popped off the lid and took a seat on the couch, letting out a hearty sigh as I brought the television to life, and confirmed that those jerks, the Quill Boars, were suffering a pounding at the hands of the Roosters. All was right in the world.

CHAPTER 3
DREA

THERE IS SUCH A THING AS TOO MUCH SLANKET

The funny thing about small towns was that while you always felt like things should be close by, everything took forever to get to down little two-lane country roads. The drunken psychic's place was no different. And despite what Paige said, she was not on the way home.

We trundled along the twisty little roads between Straddler's and the psychic's in the humid darkness of the late-May night, the three of us cool inside the air-conditioned bubble of my car.

"Ooh, there it is!" Paige shouted from the back, leaning forward between the two front seats and pointing at the little cottage tucked away at the side of the road.

"Got it," I said.

"Hard to miss though, really," April noted. She was referring to the enormous neon sign in the adjacent lot that was a likeness of the psychic winking and nodding above an arrow that pointed to her little house and the word PSYCHIC burning a hole in the darkness of the night.

I pulled into the driveway behind a new model Volvo SUV. The psychic was doing okay, I guessed.

"Here goes nothing," I muttered, switching off the engine and opening my door. The outdoor air had me wide awake and somewhat trepidatious. After all, we were bothering an older woman after ten p.m. on a Saturday night. "Are we sure she'll be open at this hour?" I asked.

"The sign is on," April pointed out.

"She would definitely switch it off if she wasn't open," Paige agreed.

That was probably true.

"Come on," April said, approaching the wide steps that led up to the front porch.

We stepped up to the front door, and just as I was about to press the doorbell, the door swung inward, revealing a woman who was probably in her late sixties with salt and pepper dreadlocks piled into a messy bun on top of her head. She wore a bulky dress that hid most of her figure and a wide smile that glowed beneath round spectacles. "Hello girls."

"How'd you know we were here?" Paige asked, eyes wide. "We didn't even ring the bell yet."

April elbowed her sister-in-law. "She's psychic, remember?"

"Ohhhh." Paige hiccuped and then was quiet.

"A reading then?" The psychic looked right at me as she asked this, and a chill shot through me. How did she know we were here for me?"

"Yes please," I said. "I mean, if you're still open. It's pretty late, and we don't want to bother you."

"No bother," she said. "I knew you were coming. Follow me. Shut the door if you would, don't want Bruno getting out."

"Oh, do you have a kitty cat?" Paige asked.

"Bruno is a feline, yes, but he's not quite what you'd refer to as a kitty."

The psychic left it at that, and we exchanged glances behind her back as she led us down a brightly lit hallway to a little room off to the right with French doors. Her dress dragged on the floor behind her, and I was careful not to step on it as we trailed her into the room.

"Have a seat," she said to me, pointing to a chair drawn up to a small table. "And you ladies can sit there." An antique couch rested against one wall, and Paige and April headed for it.

"I'm just going to"—the psychic had begun pulling the hem of her dress up, and at this point was engulfed in the bulky fabric, head and arms no longer visible—"if I could just get this thing off." Her voice was muffled from within the giant garment, and I was relieved to see she wore jeans and a T-shirt beneath it.

"Is that a Snuggie?" Paige asked the writhing mass of fleece in the center of the room. The psychic seemed to be having difficulty.

"Do you need help?" I asked.

"Yes please, if you don't mind."

I helped pull the enormous dress off over her head, and she took it from my arms and rolled it up, dropping it at one side of the room and then patting her hair. "Not a Snuggie," she said. "I went off brand, and let me tell you, big mistake."

"A Slanket?" Paige tried again.

"Not even. This is a Blafghan I got on the Home Shopping Show, and I cannot recommend it. They made the arm and neck holes too small, and if you manage to get the thing on, you're practically a prisoner inside it until someone can rescue you. Yet another peril of living on one's own."

I exchanged wide-eyed glances with April as I sank into the chair the psychic had indicated was for me. Was I doomed to find myself trapped inside an infomercial blanket dress at some point in my future? With multitudes of not-kitty cats roaming around me?

"Now sit, and let's find out why you can't snag yourself a man," the psychic said. "I might just have a little spritz." She lowered herself into a leather desk chair opposite me and turned to a mini fridge behind her, extracting a wine cooler.

"They still make those?" I remembered my mother waxing nostalgic about Bartles and Jaymes, so I'd categorized wine coolers along with sarsaparilla and Ovaltine—drinks that I'd heard of but didn't think I'd run across in the store any time soon.

"Of course they do," the psychic said, shaking her head. She downed half the wine cooler and placed it on the table to one side, and then leaned over and opened a drawer. She waved her hand, palm down over the drawer, and closed her eyes, extracting a deck of cards after a moment. "Yep, I figured." She said this to herself as she began to shuffle the deck between her hands. "The cats like you," she said to me, and I realized she had a deck of cat tarot cards. "Not a good sign if you're looking for romance."

"Wonderful," I said.

"You!" The psychic barked suddenly, glaring over at the couch.

Paige and April both jolted to upright positions as if they'd been chastised in church for slouching.

"Clap your hands, please. Twice."

April looked terrified suddenly, and she did as directed. The lights in the room immediately dimmed.

"Clap on," Paige giggled. "Clap off."

"And they call me the drunken psychic? Do they call you the drunken doctor?" The psychic delivered this in a dry tone, and I sensed I was about to get a no-nonsense reading. She was not the bumbling nut I'd expected, though she did seem to have an affinity for products sold on infomercials.

"How did she know?" Paige whispered loudly. "She is really good."

"I am," the psychic confirmed, "but you're also one of three family doctors in town. It's not a stretch that people might recognize you. Plus, I know your mother."

"Lottie," Paige muttered, as if her mother was the root of all evil. In reality, she was a nice lady who owned the Muffin Tin in downtown Singletree, and who made the best pumpkin muffins I'd ever had. Lottie was also my boss.

"Shall we get on with it?" The psychic asked me.

"Um, sure."

"Fifty."

I felt the confusion draw my brows lower. "Fifty?"

"Readings are fifty dollars. You can Venmo me or I take Zelle."

Just then, a loud yowl screeched down the hallway, echoing from somewhere deep inside the house. Fear pricked a line down my neck and arms, raising each hair, one at a time. "What was that?" My voice was unfamiliarly tiny.

"That's Bruno." The psychic seemed unconcerned. "Take these." She handed me the deck of cat tarot cards. "Close your eyes and shuffle them. Infuse them with your being."

If that was a direction I was meant to follow, I was doomed. I did not know how to infuse anything with my being. But I tried, shuffling the cards between my hands.

"Yep, good. Now think about what you want to know. The cats will answer."

I continued moving the cards between my hands and focused my mind on the one thing in my life that wasn't going the way I'd like it to: my love life. I was considering moving away, maybe heading up to Washington DC or a bigger city in Virginia where there might be more eligible men, but I loved Singletree and didn't really want to leave my dad alone here. I just needed a man to magically appear.

I guessed if it was magic I needed, tarot couldn't hurt.

"Cut the deck." The psychic's voice cut into my deliberations.

I did as I was told.

"Place the deck in the center of the table."

After a moment, the psychic began laying cards out across the table, face down, setting up a cross shape with four cards to the side of it. She gave me a meaningful look, staring at me with bright clear eyes for a beat longer than I would have liked, and then she turned back to the cards.

"The current situation," she said, moving her hand over the cross in front of me. "Past to future," her hand drifted left to right. "Subconscious to consciousness," her hand moved bottom to top.

Well, that wasn't helpful at all.

But then something crazy happened. She began flipping over cards, revealing cats in various poses with Roman numerals and strange words on the cards, and she talked in a soft voice all the while.

The things she said, and the cards she turned over made it seem like she'd read some kind of personal history of mine, or my journals, and it was enough to make me a believer.

"You are in a holding pattern. Stuck," she told me. "But an upsetting force is moving into your path. What you choose to do with this is up to you, but it will put you on a new path, no matter what you decide."

The upsetting force she spoke of was represented by the Tower, a card she said shouldn't be interpreted as negative, despite the images of cats falling (or being flung?) from a tower against a background of darkness.

"The Empress is here," the psychic went on, even though I was still picturing myself being flung from a tall tower. A white cat sat primly with a heart at her feet, moon phases scattered in an arc over her head. "In this position, she symbolizes readiness for something new."

At the end of the reading, she flipped a card called The Hierophant.

"What's a Hierophant?" Paige stage-whispered, earning her a sharp look from the psychic.

"The Hierophant sees all, knows all," she said. "And she symbolizes ritual and ceremony, as well as rules." The psychic's eyes landed on my face as her hand hovered over a winking grey cat with doves over its head. "Is your lover going to propose?" She asked, then seemed to dismiss this idea. "No. Nothing so traditional. Is he moving in?"

"I don't have a lover," I reminded her. Maybe she was drunk after all. "That is the issue."

She nodded, looking calm, as if the universe was speaking to her.

"A change, then. A symbolic and very real change, and it is up to you to embrace or deny it. It could lead you down a path that results in everything you want. A promising and fulfilling relationship that will not be without struggle." She pointed at the three of swords, showing a heart pierced by three swords hovering above a white cat.

I shivered.

"He is already in your life, this partner," she told me, squinting across the table in the low light.

There was literally no one in my life who I would consider a partner. This was when I decided the wine cooler had gone to this lady's head. "What name do I Venmo?" I asked.

She shook her head. "You will deny him at first."

"Is it an email address then?" I asked, poking at my phone.

"You are afraid of love and you will choose conflict at first. The question is whether you can step off the rutted path you walk and accept the possibility of a future you cannot envision."

"Okay then."

"Drunkenpsychic. All one word."

"So you actually call yourself the drunken psychic?" April piped up.

"Why fight it?" The woman asked with a wink.

I paid her, and then listened to April and Paige analyze my reading as I drove them home. I dropped April off last, pulling up in the circular drive in front of the old plantation house where she lived with her husband, Callan.

"Are you okay?" she asked.

"I'm exactly where I was before I paid a lady in a Snuggie fifty bucks for absolutely no reason."

April smiled sadly. "I had fun."

"Me too."

I arrived in front of my duplex a few minutes later, the familiar comfort of the river at its back settling through me as I stepped out of the car. I loved the sound of the water, the familiarity of my little house in the woods.

Only, there was a car I didn't recognize here in my second spot. A flashy black SUV, all shiny and covered with chrome.

I figured my neighbor must've had a visitor who didn't know which side to park on. Oh well, didn't matter. I only had one car anyway.

I climbed the steps to the front door, turned my key in the lock, and pushed it open, but then quickly pulled it shut again after a stream of expletives ejected themselves noisily from my lips.

Shock and fear raced through me as I tried to process what I'd just seen inside my house. The scent of pizza still surrounded me, as it had rushed out the door when I'd pushed it open.

I pulled out my phone and texted April.

> Me: There is a naked man on my couch!

> April: Your lucky day!

> Me: I'm scared!

> April: What's he doing?

> Me: He's sleeping

There, inside the front door of my apartment, asleep on my living room couch in front of the blaring television, had been a very naked man.

> April: Was he hot?

> Me: I don't know. I ran back outside. I was in shock.

> April: What are you going to do?

> Me: I guess I'm going to wake him up.

I dialed April's number and greeted her in a whisper. "I'm going in."

"I'm here."

And then I pushed open my front door and stepped inside quietly, shocked all over again by the naked man sprawled on my couch. Only this time, I wasn't shocked that he was there. I was shocked that of all the couches in Singletree, this completely perfect specimen of naked manhood happened to land on mine.

Sure, he could still be a psycho killer, but that didn't take away one little bit from the fact that the guy in front of me snoring lightly as a hockey game screamed out of the television in front of him could have been the star of a classic painting.

Muscled legs, sculpted abs that I could count if I peered closely enough, miles of golden skin covered with a light smattering of fine blond hair. Lips that were just full enough, but not too full to be masculine, and a chiseled jaw that showed hints of that same blond hair in a light stubble.

The other parts down below also appeared more than adequate, but I wasn't going to stand here meat-gazing a potential serial killer. Still... impressive.

It was time to wake him up.

I steeled myself and then reached out one finger to press between his perfectly molded pecs.

"Um, hello?"

CHAPTER 4
ROCK

RISE AND SHINE

I t had been a long day. Hell, it had been a long couple of years, up at dawn to work out, all-day practice, and in bed later than I should have been. Wash and repeat for a couple years, and you might understand how a guy falls asleep naked on a couch.

For one thing, I like walking around naked.

For another, I was actually halfway between the shower and the kitchen when I realized the Quill Boars had scored while I was in the bathroom getting ready to shower, and I ended up sitting down for a minute to watch the Roosters pound them back into the ice.

But I was sleepy.

Still, the last thing I expected was to be awakened in my own apartment by... well, by anyone. It was my apartment. Granted, there were a few random items here and there that certainly did not belong to me, but I was too tired and too used to Aunt Nattie's strange ways to think much about any of it.

I was dreaming about mashing Elliot Neville's bearded face into the glass—he was my biggest rival and I often had triumphant dreams where I took revenge for him tripping me as I was about to score in last year's championship game —but my dream ended abruptly.

With a very pointy finger in my chest and very wide eyes staring down at me. I saw these eyes, a startling shade of blue, through the one eye I popped open as the finger repeatedly jabbed at me.

In a flash, I grabbed the intruder's pointy finger and held her in place. "Who are you?" I asked, my voice rough with sleep and irritation.

"Uh. Um. Now, hang on just a second!" She snatched her finger from my grasp and took a few steps back as I sat up and rubbed my eyes. "You're the one in my apartment, so I am the one who will be asking questions. Who are you?"

"Rock Stevens."

My name seemed to confuse the intruder. Her dark brown brows drew together, and her full pink lips pulled down into a frown. Then, irritatingly, she asked. "Rock? That's your name?"

"Not the point here, sweetheart." This woman, though definitely falling somewhere close to the better end of the attractiveness spectrum, was missing the point. "What are you doing in my house?"

"My house?"

"My house, like I said." I rose to stand, and realized at that moment that I was one hundred percent naked. And even though it wasn't morning, certain parts of me were wholly faithful to the idea that upon rising, one should, uh... rise.

I turned and snatched a throw pillow off the couch, wondering as I did so where Aunt Nattie had gotten this pink furry pillow. Was it supposed to be fake fur? What kind of animal was longhaired and pink? What a strange choice of pillow.

"Don't put my pillow on your junk!" The woman leaned forward as if to snatch the faux fur monstrosity from my hands and then thought better of it, stepping back and managing to look offended.

"My pillow," I said, holding it firmly. "Well, not mine. I don't even know what kind of animal this might have been." I stared down at the pillow.

The intruder was also staring at it, a look that could only be a mixture of horror, disgust, and confusion aimed at the spot where I held it nestled against my impressive lower region.

"This has been fun," I said. "But if you just go ahead and go, I won't have to call the police."

"You?" she shrieked. Then she lifted her hand to her ear, and I realized she held a phone. "Did you hear that?" she asked the phone.

"Wait. Who are you talking to?"

"The police!" she said, her eyes widening. Then, to the phone, "yes, he's still naked."

I dropped the pillow and headed for the bathroom, where I'd left my shorts, and returned, tugging them on as she continued to describe the situation into the phone.

"He put on shorts."

"Do the police really care if I'm wearing shorts?"

"Yes, because they will add indecent exposure to the multiple counts of breaking and entering, and fearful incitement, and..." she trailed off as she searched mentally for more made-up charges.

"Fearful incitement is not a thing."

"Look, Mr. Naked Guy on My Couch, this has all been super weird, but if you could just go ahead and leave, I promise I won't file charges."

"If you want to get technical, you're the one breaking and entering."

"I have a key!" She held up a key chain that also had a pink fluffy thing attached to it. But more importantly, it had a key. The same key I had on my keyring. And I knew immediately that she'd gotten it legitimately because it looked exactly like mine. Aunt Nattie loved picking out the "fun" keys at the hardware store and she'd been in a Pokémon phase when she'd selected the keys for this rental, evidently.

I walked to the entry table where I'd dropped my keys and picked them up, holding up my own Pikachu key.

Her eyes widened and she said into the phone, "he has a Pikachu key." She paused. "I'll ask him."

Then she lowered the phone and eyed me suspiciously. "Who owns this unit?"

"Nattie Trousseau," I told her. "My aunt."

She frowned, speaking into the phone again. "He says Nattie is his aunt." Her frown deepened as the police evidently said something on the other end. "He said his name was Rock, if you can believe that."

A shriek came from the police person on the other end of the intruder's phone. Very unofficial sounding, if you asked me. But I had that effect on hockey fans.

She listened again when the shriek had subsided, and her frown deepened. "You're a hockey player?" she asked me.

I nodded, crossing my arms over my chest and straightening.

"Figures," she muttered. "I hate hockey. What a pointless game."

"Those are fighting words, missy."

"April, seriously," she said into the phone. "I think I've got this. Yeah, tell Callan to relax. Okay, thanks."

"Who is Callan? And are you on a first name basis with the cops? You find naked men in your house a lot?" I was beginning to find this situation very amusing. And the fact she'd just shit-talked the one thing that mattered to me in the world had made me want to mess with her a bit.

She shoved the phone into her jeans pocket. The jeans she wore were tight, something I let myself notice properly now. They clung to very long curvy legs accentuated by some pretty fancy high shoes. I guessed if you were going to get robbed or killed, if the intruder looked like this it was better than the alternatives. Though I could subdue this particular intruder with one hand and my eyes closed.

Which gave me a few ideas, and had things rising again down below. She was sexy in a very frustrated kind of way. But this probably wasn't the time.

"Could you just get out?"

Definitely not the time.

"Nope. My place. I pay rent." I wasn't giving in on this.

"I also pay rent."

I shook my head. That didn't make sense. Although... it did explain the weird assortment of crap in the refrigerator.

"Hang on, so those weird Icelandic yogurts in there... you bought those?"

"You ate my yogurt?" She actually stamped her little foot and threw her fists to her sides. Adorable.

"Won't happen again, I promise. Icelandic, are they? I've got a new slogan for them: Taste the Sadness of Iceland."

"They're organic and high in protein."

"High in yuk."

She blew out a breath and shook her head, sending all those dark waves of hair flying. I stepped back over to the couch and sat down. The Quill Boars were down by two now, and all felt right with the world. "Want a beer?" I lifted my forgotten bottle in invitation.

"No! Don't drink that. You're not staying!"

"My house."

"Oh my god." She sank down into the armchair next to the couch. "I'm way too tired for this. Let's call Nattie."

"It's midnight. That would be very inconsiderate." I finished my beer in a long swallow.

"It's very inconsiderate of you to break into my house, watch my television naked, and refuse to leave when I get home!"

I sighed. She was cute, but not very bright. "What's your name, anyway?"

"Drea Coppersmith."

"Short for Andrea?"

She nodded, looking adorable and exasperated all at once.

"Listen, Drea." I had a plan. "I'm not going anywhere tonight, but I think we've established that I'm not a rapist or a murderer and I'm not here to steal your weird pink fake fur pillows."

Her frown deepened as I maligned the pillows she'd clearly chosen.

"I'm Rock Stevens, the center for the Wilcox Wombats, and my aunt is Nattie Trousseau. I lived here before I moved to Wilcox, and I still pay rent on the place. I'm guessing she's double-dipping, figuring I wouldn't be back, but we can definitely get it all worked out tomorrow."

Drea leaned back in the chair, looking defeated as she blew out a long breath.

"For now, how about we both just call it a night, and we'll figure it out in the morning?"

She nodded, looking miserable. "But I get the bedroom," she said.

"Ummm, no."

She sat upright and glared at me.

"Big pickleball tourney this week. I need my rest."

The girl actually rolled her eyes. "Be a gentleman. It seems like a foreign concept to you, but it's the least you can do."

"The least I could do would be to kick your ass out of my house right now and send you to sleep at the police station with April and Callan, who do not sound like very professional members of law enforcement, by the way."

"Please?" Her voice was very small when she asked this.

"I just want a door that locks. I don't know you, and while this might all just be a misunderstanding... I'm tired, and I'm a little scared, and—"

"Fine." Dammit. She said she was scared. No one should be scared of me unless I was wearing skates and there was a puck around. "Fine. I'll sleep on the couch."

"Really?"

I nodded and leaned back to watch the end of the game.

"Thanks. Good night."

With that, Drea disappeared down the hallway and I didn't see her again until sunlight streamed in through the windows, picking up sparkling threads in the area rug I hadn't noticed the night before. Sparkles. Of course.

CHAPTER 5
DREA

A SIGNIFICANT LACK OF BACON

I slept surprisingly well, considering there was an enormous and infuriatingly stubborn stranger in my house. I supposed I could have offered him a blanket or a pillow, since I'd made him sleep on the couch, though he hadn't seemed to need one before. And he probably knew where they were kept.

When sunlight slashed across the dark grey comforter on my bed, I rolled over and stretched, as the events of the previous night came back to me one by one.

Paige and April at Straddlers, listening to me whine about being alone. The psychic and her ridiculous fortune. *He is already in your life...* the only man already in my life had been Rock Stevens of the ridiculous name and impressive physique, asleep naked on my couch as the psychic read my cards.

I mean.

There was no way she meant him. The fact that I even thought about it was annoying, and I forced the consideration from my mind. It wouldn't do to approach my intruder this morning with any vague notion that he was supposed to be anything beyond a handsome annoyance.

I sighed and sat up, hoping an upright posture would banish strange wistful thinking about naked strangers and fortunes. And I wished, not for the first time, that I had a bathroom attached to the bedroom. But as things were, I would have to leave the bedroom to do what needed doing this morning.

As I opened the door a crack, the scent of breakfast floated temptingly down the hallway. Bacon? And baked goods? Was this guy baking in my kitchen? And... was he humming? I thought I recognized the tune. It was from a musical. Rock was into Broadway? Hmm.

I tiptoed to the bathroom and slipped in, locking the door and turning on the shower, letting out a sigh of relief that I hadn't bumped into him in the hallway.

While I showered, I thought about the man in my house. Maybe he was trying to make amends for scaring me by cooking me breakfast. Maybe we could start over, figure this out like civil adults. He'd offered an olive branch by making breakfast. I could be a bigger person and try to be nice this morning, even if the whole situation was extremely weird.

Nattie would no doubt find somewhere else for him to stay, and I could get back to my regular life, which consisted mostly of lonely nights in this apartment and worrying about whether I needed to grow up and get a real job, something I'd been thinking for a while.

Dressed and cleaned up, I lifted my chin and ventured

into the kitchen, expecting to see a spread of breakfast foods and a contrite intruder. Instead, the kitchen was a disaster, and there wasn't a speck of bacon to be seen.

Rock, thankfully wearing clothes—or at least the same pair of shorts he'd had on the night before—sat at my little round table, drinking coffee and staring at his phone. He didn't even look up when I walked in, which was annoying because I might have put a little extra effort into my hair and makeup. Not for him, of course.

"Good morning," I said.

"Morning," he said, still staring at his phone. I gazed around the disaster that was my kitchen. "Did you make breakfast?"

"Yup."

I frowned. He was still staring at his phone, making no move to help me find the bacon that smelled so delicious my stomach was screaming for it. "Is there bacon?"

Rock finally turned to look at me, his eyes shifting from passive to something darker as he took me in. "Ah... there was."

"You didn't make any for me?" That was annoying. And the fact that the morning light was catching the smattering of fine blond hair on his very substantial chest and high-lighting every single muscle in his enormous arms did not make up for a lack of bacon.

"It's not like you're a guest here," he said. "I assumed you'd make whatever you wanted when you got up."

I swung my gaze around the kitchen again, spotting the coffee pot. At least there was coffee. Of course, Rock was using my favorite mug, a wide thick-walled cup in the shape of a porcupine that said, "Stick 'em Up," on it.

"You're using my mug."

Rock turned to look at me over the kitchen island, which was now strewn with bowls and spoons. "Let me ask you a question. Drea, was it?"

"Yes, ROCK." I sneered his stupid name.

"Was this place furnished when you moved in?"

I crossed my arms. "Well, yes."

"Then is any of this stuff actually yours?"

I stiffened. "I live here. It's mine."

"Well," he said, lifting his phone to his face again. "Before you lived here, it was all mine. And this is my favorite mug."

"Did you make muffins?" I hated the tiny plea in my voice, but whatever he'd made smelled fantastic. He could give Lottie Tanner a run for her money.

"I did," he said, again not offering me any.

"Are there any left?"

"Nope."

"You ate a dozen muffins?" I asked him, incredulous. When he didn't answer, I huffed out a frustrated breath and poured myself a cup of coffee in my second-favorite mug. This one was a Wilcox Wombats mug with a ferocious wombat on skates on one side.

I carried it to the table even though all I really wanted was to do was get as far away from this arrogant jerk as possible.

"That's a nice mug."

Something in the way he was smirking at me made me

want to bash his face in with the mug. Mug him with a mug. I sipped my coffee, and then realized why he'd said it.

"Oh, is this your team?"

He smiled, those full sculpted lips pulling slowly into a sexy grin that had every part of me at war internally. He was so hot. It was just so unfortunate that he was such a jerk.

"Have you called your aunt?" I asked, returning my mind to the issue at hand.

"Whenever you're ready, we'll pay her a visit." He was back to staring at his phone.

"What? I'll just call her." I stood to retrieve my own phone.

"I will need to visit with my family while I'm here anyway, and figured we could see her in person and get this all settled. I heard she was buying an inn, you know. You could probably stay there."

Fury created a loud rushing sound in my ears. "I live here," I screeched, emphasizing the *live* part of that state-ment. "You're here for a week, to play a made-up sports game, and then you're going back to wherever you came from. You stay at an inn!"

Rock sighed, like I was tiring him out.

I wanted to kill him.

I also kind of wanted to see what it would be like to rub my hands over his chest or maybe sprinkle him with powdered sugar and lick it off, thanks to his ongoing shirt-lessness.

"Fine," I said, sinking back down to drink my coffee.

"Are you going to put on a shirt at least? Or clean up this mess?"

"Doesn't Wanda still come by on Saturdays?"

"Wanda?"

"My cleaning lady."

I shook my head. "No Wanda."

He looked exceptionally put out by this news. "We'll deal with all that later. I'm going to take a shower. Don't eat the muffins."

I could feel the steam gathering inside me. This man was impossible. "You said there were no muffins left."

"Technically there are. But they're for my aunt, not for the random chick squatting in my house."

"I am not squatting. I pay rent."

"We'll see." He rose and headed for the bathroom, in no particular hurry, leaving me to watch his back ripple as he walked away from me.

I tried not to do it, but a mess was something I couldn't abide, and I found myself cleaning up the kitchen as I waited for Rock to finish his shower.

He emerged from the bathroom fifteen minutes later, a towel slung low around his waist.

"Oh my god!" I said, turning partially away as he whipped the towel off despite me still being in the kitchen. "Do you ever wear clothes?"

"I'm getting dressed right now. Not my fault you decided the living room would be my bedroom. Why are you watching if it bothers you so much?"

Oh god, he was right. I was watching him bend down to retrieve clothes from the duffel bag on the floor. I snapped my eyes away, spinning to face the window over the kitchen sink.

Why was this happening to me?

A moment later, Rock stood at my side, smelling clean and manly, and towering above me in a way that kind of made me want to lean into all that infuriating strength. "Ready when you are."

"Yes. Let's go figure this out."

"I'll drive."

Because of course he would.

"Fine."

Rock pulled a basket of muffins from the oven and handed them to me. "You hold these. Don't eat them."

I made a face at him and followed him out to his stupid shiny SUV, trying not to admire how clean and new it was.

And then Rock drove us over to Nattie's like a guy who'd lived in Singletree his whole life. A really annoyingly sexy guy.

CHAPTER 6

ROCK
COME ON INN

I was almost sorry my time with Drea was coming to an end. I was certain Aunt Nattie would give her another place to stay and she'd be out of my hair.

It had been fun watching her little face pull itself into a variety of adorably exasperated expressions during our short time together. I also didn't mind the sexy little pout she kept putting on.

Actually, there was a lot about Drea that was pretty sexy, not the least of which was the fact that she smelled a little bit like cinnamon, my personal catnip.

We pulled up to Aunt Nattie's old Victorian house, and I spotted my cousin, Noah, coming around from the back.

"Noah, what's good, man?" I jumped down from the car to greet him. We'd grown up together. Noah had a bunch of brothers, and sometimes I thought Aunt Nattie just counted me as another son. My own family hadn't been terribly attentive, so I'd spent most of my time here.

"Didn't know you were in town," Noah said. He grinned

at me, but his face shifted as he glanced over my shoulder and spotted Drea coming around the front of the car. "Who's this?" he asked.

"This is the lady who's squatting in my apartment."

Noah managed to almost suppress his look of surprise.

"She has muffins," he pointed out.

"I made those," I said, taking the muffins from Drea. "They're for your mom."

"Aha," he said. "I'm Noah," he told Drea.

"Drea," she said, her voice sweet and light. Not the voice she used with me.

"Uh, Noah, what's going on here? The place looks a little rough." Parts of Aunt Nattie's house were laying on the ground, and other parts seemed in need of paint. As if they were taking it apart and reassembling it like a Lego house. There was a toilet and a stove in the center of the lawn.

"We're renovating. Mom has this crazy idea that she can turn this place into a bed and breakfast."

"I thought she was buying an inn or something?"

"Or something. It's a little bit nuts, man."

Aha. Not buying an inn, then. Making her own house into an inn. The place did have like four million rooms, or it had seemed that way growing up.

"Hey, come on in," Noah said. "I think Mom's around here somewhere."

Noah led us up the porch and through the front door, and the familiar scent of Aunt Nattie's place washed over me, hitting me with a dose of nostalgia big enough to rattle me a bit. I'd been happy here as a kid. Life was always better at Aunt Nattie's.

"Mom?" Noah called, his voice echoing through the cavernous front entry way and up the staircase to one side.

"This place is amazing," Drea said, looking around.

"Ohh, it will be!" Aunt Nattie's voice came from around the corner of what she had always called the drawing room, and she emerged, her silver hair tied up in a bandanna, and white smears across her cheeks and down her arms. "A lot of paint and elbow grease required!" She smiled widely as her eyes landed on me.

"Hello, Aunt Nattie."

"Rock Stevens! You're a sight for sore eyes." She threw herself at me, giving me a hug that made me feel like a kid again, except that I was about two feet taller than my aunt, so I had to lean down to return it.

Aunt Nattie stepped back and turned to Drea. "Oh! And you've met Drea!" Her smile widened further, and her light eyes danced. "Are the two of you... an item?"

"No!" Drea practically shouted it, and if I hadn't had such a healthy sense of self-esteem, it might have hurt my feelings a bit. Was it so far-fetched that she might go out with me?

Would I go out with her?

I'd be lying if I said I hadn't noticed the way her sexy little smile teased at the side of her pretty pink lips, or the way her tight little waist gave way to a very voluptuous backside that I might have thought about a little more than I should.

"We are actually here to settle a dispute," I told my aunt. "But first, muffins." I nodded at Drea, who had taken back the basket of muffins and held it in front of her, and now she held them out to my aunt, her eyes narrowing at me.

"Ooh, are these from the Muffin Tin, Drea? Did you make them?"

"No, they're from my house, actually. Rock made them." Noah gave me a questioning look at this news, and Drea muttered, "and wouldn't let me have one and then didn't bother to clean up after himself."

"What happened to Wanda?" I asked my aunt.

"Oh dear," she said, seeming to understand a bit more than we'd told her about the situation at hand. "Let's take these into the kitchen and figure this all out, shall we?"

"If we had a kitchen, that would be easier," Noah said.

"We have a kitchen," Aunt Nattie said, leading us down the hallway and taking a left turn into what I remembered as the kitchen. Only this room had been gutted almost completely. A refrigerator stood to one side, and a sink was still hooked up beneath the window overlooking the backyard and the riverbank. Everything else seemed to have been removed, and there were piles of discarded tile and a bank of disassembled cabinets on the floor. In the center of it all was the kitchen table I practically grew up at, eight chairs flanking the enormous wooden structure.

"Sit down!" Aunt Nattie instructed us. "Coffee?"

"Uh, sure," I said, wondering how she planned to make coffee. Aunt Nattie went to the discarded cabinets leaning against the wall and scrounged through one until she emerged again with a coffee machine, which she sat on the floor and plugged into an outlet that looked a lot like a fire hazard.

"That'll just be a minute," she told us, taking a muffin and then seating herself next to Noah. "Now, to what do we owe the pleasure?"

"I came home last night to find this man naked on my couch!" Drea had evidently been holding that in for a while, because it came out forcefully. With a lot of rage. It was kind of hot, actually.

"And I was peacefully dozing on my own couch watching the game, when this hooligan broke into my house and began making demands."

"Hooligan?" Noah asked, chuckling.

"Oh dear," Aunt Nattie said, sounding as if she'd been caught at something. "I'm so sorry, kids. This is my fault."

"Aunt Nattie," I said. "I have been paying rent all this time. Did you rent out my house to someone else? With all my things still in it?"

"Well, when you put it that way, it sounds just terrible."

"Mom!" Noah looked horrified as he grabbed a muffin from the basket and pulled off the paper. "He's family. You're double dipping?"

"No, no," she said. "It isn't like that. I didn't mean to." She squinted her eyes and put her hands to her forehead like her next thought hurt her. "Drea, darling. Can you tell me please. Is there anyone living in the unit next to you?"

"Yes," Drea said. "Mr. Mulligan. And about forty cats."

"Oh dear," Aunt Nattie said.

"Mom, seems like you'd better explain now," Noah said.

"Or," I suggested, "you give little Drea here a room at your inn, and we're good."

"Little?" Drea fumed. "And no, that would make nothing

good. That would still be bad. You're family. You stay at the inn." She turned to my aunt and Noah. "Sorry. I didn't mean to yell. This..." she searched for a word. "This *person* is infuriating." She made a face at me as she called me a person that had me doing my best to stifle a giggle. She was adorable. And "person" was her worst insult?

God, I suddenly wanted to take her to bed. Part of it was that I hated it when people didn't like me. I was a delightful person when you got to know me. A bigger part of it was that I didn't like it when women didn't like me. As a rule, women usually liked me. A lot. But most of the issue was that there was something about this particular woman that had started to get under my skin. Maybe it was simply that she didn't like me. It was novel. Curious.

"No one can stay at the inn," Noah informed us. "Every room upstairs looks about like this."

"Ohh, coffee's ready!" Aunt Nattie seemed to have recovered from whatever realization she'd had, but hadn't shared it with us so far. She poured coffee, offered us cream and sugar, and then sat back down.

"Well," she said. "There's nothing for it until I can get Mr. Mulligan out."

"I don't understand," Drea said.

"My mistake, dear," Aunt Nattie said. "I meant to rent you the other side. Mr. Mulligan's side. He stopped paying rent and told me he was leaving, but I suppose I never really made sure. I sent Wanda in there to clean the place, thinking I'd been very clear that someone new was moving in, but she must have gotten confused. Rock, you were gone, see, and so... she just put you in the wrong side, dear," she told Drea. Aunt Nattie shrugged as if this was no big deal.

"I've been living in the wrong apartment for six months?" Drea asked, one hand pressed to her chest, a gesture that had my mind going places that were wholly inappropriate for coffee and muffins with one's aunt.

"This Mulligan guy needs to leave," I said. "Easy as that."

"Right," Aunt Nattie said, only she didn't sound sure. "It's just that, well, he's a bit of a character." This, coming from the biggest character I knew.

"Who's been living rent free for six months and didn't bother to mention it. Did he live there when I did?" I asked.

Aunt Nattie nodded.

"I've never seen the guy. Or heard him." That was strange.

"Me either," Drea said. "I mean, I've seen the cats."

Noah sighed. "Mom thinks he's a vampire."

I spit out my coffee. "Sorry," I said, wiping at the table with a paper towel. "What now?"

"When he moved in, there was a, erm... a, well. He sleeps in a coffin." Aunt Nattie looked embarrassed by this news.

"Why'd you rent to this guy?" I asked her.

"He sent a proxy," Noah explained. "A fancy lawyer guy who made all kinds of stipulations but promised he would never be a problem in any way."

"Uh, that rent thing seems like an issue," I pointed out.

"Mom, do you still have the lawyer's info?"

"I do," she said, rising and looking dramatically around

the ruined kitchen as if it might be poking from between two destroyed tiles. "Somewhere."

"In the meantime," I said. "I need my place. I have a big pickleball tournament this week."

Drea actually snickered.

"I'm sorry," I said, turning to her. "Do you find my job amusing?"

"Wait," she said, stifling another chuckle. "I thought you played hockey?"

"I do. It's an all-star game. They're paying me to play."

"That's cool, man," Noah said. "I think Mrs. Tanner is playing in that tournament too."

"My boss? Lottie?" Drea asked.

Aunt Nattie nodded. "Lots of locals are playing. They paid some sports guys to come take on the local team. The Singletree Soup Slingers are pretty tough."

"The Sing..." I couldn't even repeat what she'd just said. I dropped my head into my hand. I wasn't even playing proper athletes? Lottie Tanner was nice, but she was pushing seventy and spent her days finding creative ways to add alcohol to baked goods. This was ridiculous.

"Sounds like you're not playing a lot of 'all stars,' so you'll be good without your usual beauty rest, champ," Drea said, and I had the urge to tackle her and tickle her until she gave in to my extreme charm. And also stopped making fun of my pickleball problem. But this was an issue. I needed her out of my house.

"You're family," Drea pointed out. "Can't Rock stay here for a week?"

"If we had a spare room, definitely," Aunt Nattie said.

"But we might have gone a bit overboard with the demolition."

"I have a tent," Noah said, looking at me.

"No way in hell," I told him. The mosquitos in Maryland were bigger than my head.

"Can't you guys just share for a few days until I get Mr. Mulligan's lawyer on the phone?"

"Or you could offer to put Drea up in a hotel until then," I suggested.

"All my stuff is at your house!" she protested.

"At least you admit it's my house."

"Oh my god, you're a child. And you're the superstar pickleball player, why don't you get a hotel? I work at a bakery. I can barely afford rent as it is!"

"Oh honey, you should have told me," Aunt Nattie said, looking worried.

Noah stood. "I'll make sure Mom gets in touch with the vampire next door, okay? In the meantime, can you guys share without anyone getting maimed?"

Drea stood too. "Can't promise anything." She'd stopped arguing, I noticed. Maybe my charm was beginning to have an effect on her.

"I can if she can," I said magnanimously. "Temporarily."

"Good!" Aunt Nattie clapped her hands together and stood too, and something about the way she was looking at me made me think she'd picked up on my attraction to my new roommate. "Maybe it'll be better than you think." She had the audacity to wink.

"It won't," Drea said drily.

"Thanks for the muffins, darlings!" Aunt Nattie said, walking us back to the front door.

"Good luck," my cousin said, chuckling.

I wasn't sure if I was going to need luck or restraint to make it through a week with Drea as my roommate. Either way, I was going to make sure that she liked me by the end of our time together.

CHAPTER 7

DREA

CATS TAKE ON NEW MEANING

Well, the visit to Nattie's solved absolutely nothing. And now I had a tall, muscly, arrogant roommate I didn't want for the foreseeable future. And all the way back to "our" house, he was giving me a weird smile.

"What?" I asked him as he guided his dumb shiny car down the winding two-lane road.

"I haven't had a roommate since college," he said, sounding weirdly gleeful.

"We are not roommates. You'll be on the couch. And you'd better not eat any more of my yogurts."

"We can get some tape and put a line down the middle of the fridge if you want. And set up a bathroom and television schedule." He said this as if he was serious, but I wasn't going to get my happy little organizationally obsessed hopes up. He was kidding.

I sniffed and looked out the window in response.

The real issue here? Besides the complete invasion of my

space and my life, it was that Rock was so stupidly attractive that I found myself wishing things were different. Why couldn't he have stayed somewhere else and then we could have bumped into each other at Straddlers or he could have wandered into the Muffin Tin?

Of course then, with my track record with stupidly attractive men, he'd never notice me at all.

Not that he'd exactly noticed me now.

Ugh. This was the problem. My brain was doing all kind of calculating and twisty-turny thinking trying to convince me that maybe if I was nice to him, Rock would look at me as something more than an inconvenience to his pickleball plans. Maybe he'd look at me like...

Like he was doing right now.

"What?" I practically shrieked.

"Just wondering if you were planning to get out of the car," he said, chuckling.

We were home. And I'd been so absorbed in delirious confusion that I hadn't even noticed.

"Of course I am," I said, my voice haughty even though I didn't want it to be. This man did things to me. Dammit.

We both stared over toward Mr. Mulligan's side of the duplex as we headed inside. My neighbor had shifted dramatically in my thoughts since last night. Now I was a teeny bit afraid, and it almost made me glad that Rock was here.

"You don't really think..."

"No way," Rock said. "Might have some odd proclivities, but we all know vampires aren't real. And if he is one, he must be into cat blood."

"That's why all the cats, you think?"

"Why else?"

I shook my head. My life had gotten really weird all of a sudden.

"What are you up to today, roomie?" Rock asked, sitting his enormous self on my couch and blinking up at me.

"Um. I have a shift this afternoon." I stood awkwardly in the center of the room, feeling like a visitor in my own home.

"So lunch then? And I can drop you off at work."

I felt myself frowning at him. "Why? Just because you're stuck here for a few days doesn't mean we have to be friends."

"Doesn't mean we can't be."

"Don't you have things to do?" I looked around me as if a stack of books labeled Things Rock Needs to Do might be laying on a tabletop.

"Nope. I'll hit the gym while you're at work. That'll give me time to make dinner."

"Oh god, please don't cook again."

It was Rock's turn to frown. "I'm an excellent cook."

"Don't you have, like, family to visit with or something?"

"We just did that."

I moved to the kitchen and poured myself another cup of coffee, sticking it in the microwave to reheat. "I mean like, immediate family? You grew up here, didn't you?"

"I did," he confirmed. "Where did you grow up?"

"I see how you avoided answering the question, but I'll let you get away with it because I'm sensing you don't want to talk about it." I took my coffee from the microwave and carried it to the table. "I grew up in Alexandria for the most part. We moved here in high school."

"Why?"

"My dad's mom was sick. He's from here. She died, and we never left."

"So your dad is here."

I nodded.

Rock seemed to think about this for a moment, then leaned forward, resting his forearms on his knees. "Where should we go for lunch? I vote for Solomon's."

The boardwalk at Solomon's Island, which wasn't really an island, had a bunch of water-facing seafood restaurants and bars. It was kind of a tourist spot—as much as tourists came down this far in Maryland. I hadn't been there in years.

"Uh, okay. But I have to be at work at one."

"No problem. We'll go now."

I looked at the clock. It was ten-thirty. "Um."

"Sunday brunch. It's a thing. Let's go. Bring your work stuff." He stood, apparently ready to go.

"Give me a minute." In the bathroom I stared into the mirror. What the hell was happening? I put on a bit of lipstick and brushed out my long dark hair, and decided to just go along with it. At least Rock had quit being a jerk.

When I stepped out of the bathroom, Rock was on the phone with someone, standing in front of the window and staring out into the dense woods as one hand scrubbed through the messy golden-brown hair atop his head.

"No, Sam. Not an all-star situation down here."

A pause.

"Oh, I get it. Well, thanks for that, but not really your business."

Another pause.

"We were friends." He said this sadly, as if this friend, Sam, had lost his trust. "I'll do it. Then I'm going to be considering new representation." He sounded angry, but as soon as he turned and saw me, he grinned. "Let's go!"

It was like Rock had suddenly become a different version of the tall, hunky naked guy I'd first discovered on my couch. He was charming and funny over brunch, and I felt a little bit like I was spending time in a parallel dimension.

"Was that your agent on the phone?" I asked him once our mimosas had arrived.

"Potentially former agent," he said, the cheer in his eyes evaporating.

"Because of the tournament?" I shouldn't have been prodding. It wasn't my business. But I was curious.

Rock looked at me for a long beat, his dark brown eyes on mine, his eyebrows lowering slightly, as if he was trying to figure something out. Then he let out a little sigh and started talking.

"Yeah," he began. "Sam is a friend really. And he just admitted on the phone that he sent me down here to this thing because he knew Singletree was my hometown. He thinks I have some things to figure out here."

"Like what? I mean besides taking care of the fact that someone else is living in your house?"

He smiled at that, and then dropped my gaze. "He

thinks I should forgive my mom for some things while I'm here, but I have no plans on doing that."

"Ohh," I said, understanding making me quieter. "Yeah, that's not his call."

"He's probably right," Rock said, sounding sad. "It's just..." his eyes met mine again and something shuttered. "Never mind. You don't want to hear about that." He took a long swallow of his drink and then grinned at me. I was beginning to see that the grin was a cover.

"You and your mom don't get along?"

"We don't speak, so no."

"And your dad?"

"Left a while ago," he said.

"Ah."

"But Drea," Rock said, leaning back as a tower of pancakes was placed in front of him and my omelet was delivered to me. "Let's talk about you."

"Um—"

"You work at the Muffin Tin, which explains why you always smell good. Tell me what else I need to know."

He thought I smelled good? He noticed how I smelled? A little thrill went through me for some reason at the idea of Rock thinking about that.

"There's really not much else. Dad is nearby, so I have no plans to leave, even though..."

"Here it comes. Tell me the dream."

"I'd like to go to culinary school."

"This is why you got so upset about the kitchen?"

"Only semi-related," I assured him. "I've always loved to

bake and cook, and working at the Tin just makes me wish it was mine."

"So your plan is to go off to learn some incredible cutting-edge culinary strategies and then open a competing bakery in Singletree?"

I laughed. "No, I don't think so. I don't really have a plan. I can't leave my dad right now."

"Because..."

"Because he's old and alone. He needs me."

Rock didn't say anything to that, and we finished our meal making small talk about the weather, the boardwalk, and what it was like living in one of Maryland's prettiest spots, remote though it was.

"Let's walk," Rock said after he insisted on paying for brunch and we found ourselves facing one another on the boardwalk outside.

I checked my watch. "I have about an hour."

"Perfect."

We walked, the late spring sun beating down on us as the salty air began to hint at the warmth of summer to come. A few other people were scattered down the length of the long wooden boardwalk, and walking by Rock's side felt strangely comfortable.

He told me about hockey, about how he'd gotten into playing, and how he'd been recruited to his team out of college. "Can't play forever, though," he said, sounding almost sad. "And I guess I'm kind of starting to think about that. About what's next."

We'd come to a stop along the edge of the walkway, and faced each other with the cement wall to our side and the sound of the water lapping beneath us as sea birds wheeled above.

"What's next?" I asked him, sensing a subtle shift in the air between us as his eyes met mine again.

"I think next," he answered slowly, his eyes dipping to my mouth and then slowly coming back up. "Next, I'd like to kiss you."

I responded without intending to, stepping closer and tilting my chin up to him, and one of Rock's enormous hands moved gently to cup my cheek, his thumb tracing the line of my jaw. And then slowly, almost painfully so, he inclined his head to meet my lips.

The kiss was tentative, at least at first. His lips were soft and gentle, and the touch on mine was just a whispered suggestion, a hint. But a tiny sound escaped me then—a mix of pleasure and disbelief—and it must have been a cue to Rock to increase the pressure.

His arms went around me, pulling me against his solid form, and I found my own hands on his back, trying to get closer to him, to increase the contact between us. His lips moved against mine, his tongue teasing until I opened to him, and he dipped the tip of his tongue into my mouth.

Sparks exploded in my mind—I'd never been kissed like this. Ever.

Rock's mouth moved expertly, coaxing, tasting, teasing me until I was practically wrapped around him, a rag doll in his grip.

Finally, he broke contact, keeping me pulled against him as he gazed down with darkened eyes. "We're going to have to stop or this is going to get out of hand. And there are children around."

That snapped me out of it, and I detached myself from his enormous form as quickly as I could. My legs were a bit shaky. "I, uh. Yeah."

"Shall I deliver you to work?" he asked, stepping back and running a big hand through his wavy hair, sending it standing on end in a very sexy sort of mess.

"Oh. Ah." I was having a hard time getting my brain to click back into place. "Yes. Thanks."

Rock drove me to The Muffin Tin, greeted Lottie with a kiss to the cheek, and then departed, leaving me with a spinning head and a bit of explaining to do.

CHAPTER 8
ROCK

DETAILS ABOUT TRANSYLVANIA

I'd done it. Drea didn't hate me. She'd kissed me, so that proved it. But what the hell was I supposed to do now?

The problem, I realized as I drove back to my house from dropping her off at work, was that I actually liked her. In a way I hadn't liked a woman in a really long time. If ever.

I knew it was ridiculous. I barely knew her.

But it didn't seem to matter to the part of my brain that insisted on fixating around the kiss we'd just shared. She'd been responsive, and soft, and the way her body had fit mine had me wondering what it would be like to continue that exploration somewhere more private. And naturally, the rest of me reminded me that we were currently sharing an apartment. Possibilities abounded.

But I also didn't want to lead her on. I didn't live here. Not really. And she sounded like she was figuring things out too.

And furthermore, I told myself as I pulled up to the duplex, I had no business even thinking about this kind of thing. I wasn't looking for entanglements. I needed to keep my head in the game. Except it wasn't. Not in hockey, and not in pickleball. Right now, it was only in one place. With Drea.

I decided I was going to let myself explore this thing—If she was on board, of course. I was here for a week. We'd see what might evolve.

I called my aunt and let her know that we'd worked things out and not to worry about Mr. Mulligan if she didn't want to. She sounded relieved. Evidently Mr. Mulligan's attorney lived in a distant part of some European country and was difficult to reach during business hours.

"Like Transylvania?" I asked her.

"Don't be ridiculous," Aunt Nattie said. "But... I think that's actually right, yes."

"Well, take your time. Things are working out over here."

"Interesting," Aunt Nattie said, catching my drift.

I hung up with her and got to work tidying the place up and getting ready to execute my plan for the evening, which I hoped involved more time spent figuring out why I wanted Drea so badly. And maybe getting to explore her curvy, cinnamon-scented body in a bit more detail.

But I was getting ahead of myself. First, dinner.

I picked Drea up after her shift, and nearly lost it when the scent of cinnamon filled the car once she was settled.

"I could have gotten a ride," she said, though she didn't sound upset. "You didn't have to drive me again."

"I like driving you," I said, struggling to stay on my side of the car. "Damn, you smell good."

She gave me a funny look then, and sighed.

"What?" I asked.

"I can't... I can't tell if you're flirting with me. Or if you're just being you. It's just..."

"I'm flirting," I assured her.

"Oh."

I navigated back toward our shared home, and explained. "Look. I'm only here a week. And I have no idea if this is insane, but I want to use that time to get to know you. To figure out if maybe there's something here besides this infatuating cinnamon scent and deeper than my ridiculous attraction to that little pout you make with your lips."

"My. Um... Rock, we just met."

"That's usually how things begin."

"But..."

Worry gripped me then. Did she not feel the same way? Was this one-sided? But the kiss had definitely not been one-sided. "Oh," I said, trying to let her off the hook.

"No, no. Now you sound sad."

"I'm not sad."

"I'm not saying no."

"You literally just said, 'no, no.'"

"But that's not what I meant."

"I take consent pretty seriously. If you say no—" I pulled into the spot in front of the house as Drea unbuckled her seatbelt.

Then she shocked me by climbing across the center console and settling herself in my lap, facing me. She took my face in her soft hands and stared into my eyes. "I'm not saying no," she whispered.

And then she kissed me in a way that I felt all the way into my toes as she moved against me, giving rise to some very impure thoughts and some very curious body parts.

I gripped her to me, letting my hands slide down her back and fill themselves with her generous curves, which elicited a breathy moan from her and a deep groan from me.

"Should we go inside?" she asked, breaking contact.

"I mean, I could work with this," I said, painfully aware that her hands had begun sliding lower as she worked the button on my shorts.

She stopped moving, took a deep breath, and then slid back to her seat. "Let's go inside. I should clean up."

We got out of the car and I unlocked the door, but caught Drea's hand before she headed to the bathroom. "Listen," I told her, making my voice stern. "You can go in there, and do whatever you need to do. But don't you dare wash that incredible smell from your skin. If you do, I'll strip you naked and sprinkle you with cinnamon to get it back."

"Kinda weird," she said, grinning. "Also, kinda hot."

She reappeared just a minute later, and wasted no time at all. She was in my arms in a second, her hands returning to my waistband.

I took her mouth again, and then groaned in partial disappointment and partial excitement as she moved her hands to my neck and wrapped a leg around me. I lifted her up and both legs went around my waist.

"Bedroom," she whispered against my lips.

I did not need to be told twice.

I laid Drea gently down on the bed, taking a moment to admire her, and to let myself enjoy the fact that I was about to have her, to feel her surrounding me, to hear what amazing sounds she made when I made her come.

Her eyes were glossy and heavy-lidded, and her lips were red and swollen. Pride filled me. I did that.

I reached for the button on her jeans, checking her face for any sign of hesitation, and then slid them from her body, leaving her panties in place. And then I settled myself between her legs, pressing them wide with my shoulders until her heels were hooked against my back. And then I dipped my head and kissed her—along each soft thigh, across the silky fabric of her panties, and finally, with the fabric still between us, I took one long languorous lick straight up her center.

Drea moaned, and her hands went into my hair.

I pushed the fabric aside and began to work, lapping and teasing, my fingers pressing and circling her sensitive nub until her legs began to shake against me and her hands were pulling my hair and pushing my head where she needed me to go.

"Oh god," she moaned. "Rock, don't stop. Please..." she didn't finish whatever incredible plea she was going to make, because her orgasm overtook her then, and I felt it in every nerve of my own body as she spasmed and writhed against my mouth and hands.

Fuck, she was gorgeous.

"Come here," she whispered, and I climbed her perfect body, holding myself over her.

"Shirt off," she demanded after kissing me long and slow. I rolled to one side and complied.

"These too," she said, pointing at my shorts. A moment later, I was fully naked, lying next to her as her breath returned to normal.

And then she moved, covering me with her body as she kissed me. My hands found the hem of her shirt and then the clasp of her bra, and the sight of Drea's incredible breasts nearly made me come.

"You're fucking perfect," I told her. I meant it. She had curves for days, enough for me to explore and fill my hands and my mind. She was solid enough I didn't worry I would hurt her, and so fucking feminine it was hard not to accelerate this entire encounter just so I could feel what it was like to be inside her.

She slid down my body, her hands taking me in a firm grip just before her hot little mouth enveloped my tip and nearly sent me over the edge.

"Oh, fuck," I managed.

And then Drea began a rhythm of sucking, pulling, and licking that stole my grasp of the English language. I became sensation only, and could only avoid letting go completely by pulling her physically off my cock and up my body.

"Not good?" she asked, lying on top of me again.

"Too fucking good," I told her. "I want to feel you. Is that okay?"

She rolled off and opened a drawer, resuming her place with a plastic packet in her hand.

I let Drea roll the condom down my length, loving every second of watching her touch me, seeing the way her breasts moved as she did. So fucking sexy.

And then she moved over me again, and my hands found her hips. She lowered herself bit by bit down my length and I gritted my teeth against the desire to pound upwards, to take her, to have this perfect girl in every way possible.

Finally, she was seated and she began to move, undulating those incredible hips in a way that had me gasping for breath. The movement morphed into a steady rhythm, and as she tossed her head back and rode me, I gave into the need to pump, to thrust, to take her rhythm and return it. And moments later, Drea cried out again, surprising me.

Her second orgasm, speared on my cock as I hovered on the edge of ecstasy myself, was so hot, I gave in. And as she finished, I began, and the sensations that rocketed through me were more powerful than anything I'd ever felt before. I saw stars, I might have passed out for a second.

"Holy shit," I managed, as Drea crumpled on top of me. I

stroked her back, let my hands tangle in the long strands of dark hair that had escaped her bun.

"Yeah," she said. And then after a minute, she sat up, sniffing. "Did you cook again?"

I nodded. "And I cleaned the kitchen too."

"Oh. For a second I thought you made me dinner." She laughed as if this was the craziest idea in the world.

"I did," I told her, earning me a surprised smile. "Let's go eat."

CHAPTER 9
DREA

WE NOW RETURN TO OUR REGULARLY SCHEDULED LIFE

There was no way I could have known that coming home to a naked man on my couch would begin the single best week of my life. Or at least the week in which I had the most sex ever.

Rock was always ready, and surprisingly, I couldn't get enough of him, either. We both did the things we needed to do, but in between, we were together. On the couch, on the island in the kitchen, on the living room rug, and in the bed more times than it was worth trying to count. But the thing was, it wasn't just sex.

It was so much more.

Rock treated me like a princess, like something he cherished and wanted to take care of. He brought me little gifts when he came home from practice. He cooked for me. He opened doors and pulled out chairs.

He took little tiny pieces of my heart, one by one, until I knew he would take the rest of it with him when he left.

Friday morning, the day before Rock's big game, we lay

in bed after yet another round of mind-melting shenanigans.

"You okay, babe?" Rock had started calling me babe. I loved it.

Something about lying in his strong arms, next to his warm, solid, muscle-bound body and hearing his voice so gentle and soft made me shiver. I pressed myself closer to him, humming my contentment.

A little while later, I glanced at the clock. "Crap. I have to get up for work."

Rock tightened his arm around me in response, keeping me there.

I squirmed, partially because it was fun to feel him trying to hold me close as I pretended to desperately want to get away, but also because I really did need to get showered and get to work.

"Rock," I laughed.

His hand slid down, his arm crossing my stomach as he flexed, pulling me on top of him. His other hand joined the first on the cheeks of my ass as he pressed me into his erection, which could also have been named Rock at that moment.

I kissed him, long and slow and sleepy, and then rolled off the bed and out of his reach.

"Big sad," Rock murmured, making me smile as I headed for the shower.

When I emerged, he was dressed and awake. "I'll take you to work," he said. "I should hit the gym anyway."

As Rock drove me to the Muffin Tin, worry tried to press in around the edges of the ridiculous happiness I'd been feeling. What would happen when he left? We really hadn't talked about whatever this was, or what we wanted. And Rock was leaving in two days to go back to Virginia.

We parked at the Tin and Rock helped me out of his big car and then walked me inside. Such a gentleman.

"Look who's here!" Nattie sat at a little round table just inside the door.

"Hey Aunt Nattie," Rock said, bending down to give her a kiss on the cheek.

"I am just so tickled at how this has all worked out," she said, making me wonder what she was talking about. "It was such a relief to get your call, Rocky, because I had no idea how I was going to get ahold of that lawyer way out there in Europe. He seems to keep the same hours as his client, and it was just so nice to hear that I didn't need to call him anyway."

I shook my head. "Mr. Mulligan's lawyer?"

Nattie nodded, and Rock stiffened slightly at my side.

"You never called him?" I wasn't sure what to make of that news. Rock had told her not to call him? Why?

"Rock told me you two were getting along just fine and not to worry about it." Nattie picked a crumb off the top of her muffin and pushed it into her mouth delicately.

"When was that?" I asked them both.

Rock didn't answer, but his aunt did. "Right after you were at my place. What was that, Rocky? Monday?"

I turned to look at Rock. "You told her not to worry about finding another place for you to stay, Rocky?" I drew out the nickname trying to stifle my anger.

He swallowed and then gave me his killer grin. "Look how it worked out."

I couldn't speak as my mind raced back through the week. Had he planned this all, then? Decided that if there was a girl in his house he might as well take advantage of the situation while he was in town? And then what?

"You might have told me," I said, lowering my voice.

"What difference did it make?" Rock's voice lowered too, and while his words weren't what I wanted to hear, I could tell he understood why I was upset.

"So what?" I hissed. "You just figured I'd be your convenient fuck buddy for the week so long as you were here? And then what? You just head on back to your regularly scheduled life in Virginia?"

"I don't know what happens at the end of the week," he said, sounding a little bit sorry, but not sorry enough. "I thought we'd talk about it tonight."

I shook my head. "I'll make it easy for you. I can stay with Paige until you're gone. I should have done that in the first place."

"Drea, no—"

"Good luck in your game," I said, anger and hurt warring for the premier spot in my chest.

Nattie looked confused at this exchange, and I could feel her eyes and Rock's on my back as I headed to the back of the Muffin Tin to hide in the kitchen.

I was assuring myself that I would not cry when I spotted Paige in the back, sitting on a tall stool with a cup of coffee in her hand and a bowl of some kind of dough in front of her.

"Hey," she said in a kind voice. "Did I just hear you announce that you're staying with me?"

"You heard that?" I said, horrified. Had I been shouting?

"Bakeries are not known for their acoustics. But Drea, what's going on? Last we talked the psychic had come through and your life was all rainbows and orgasms."

"I was wrong."

"What do you mean?"

"Rock was using me. He figured that since I was already living in his place, he might as well take advantage of the situation until he goes home."

She frowned. "He said that?"

It was my turn to frown. "No, but he called his aunt right after we asked her to help us figure the situation out and told her not to worry about it."

"Well, he should have talked to you first," Paige agreed.

"I feel so dirty. And stupid."

Paige stood and came to wrap her arms around me. "No," she said gently. "You did what you wanted for a week, lived like a strong independent woman taking what she wanted. There's no shame in that at all."

"Unless that woman thought maybe it was going to turn into something more."

Paige squeezed me. "Oh, honey."

"I'm so stupid."

"No, you're not. You're sensitive and hopeful and optimistic. There's a difference. And this guy better not have crushed that beautiful hopeful heart of yours or I'll have to make him pay for it."

I loved that my friend would stand up for me, but I felt

too heavy and sad to say much more about it. "Is it okay if I stay for a couple nights?"

"If you're okay with the girls insisting on doing your hair and makeup."

"Deal."

And then I commenced the saddest workday I'd ever spent at the Tin. Luckily, by the time I went back out front, both Rock and his aunt were gone.

CHAPTER 10

ROCK

IT BEGINS WITH FLOWERS

"Well, you really soiled the sheets on that one," Aunt Nattie told me as we left the Muffin Tin. "What are you going to do?"

I shook my head, still trying to figure out what happened in there. All I really knew was that I'd screwed up, and one of the best things that had ever happened to me suddenly hated me. "Not sure. She hates me."

"She doesn't hate you," Aunt Nattie said, steering me for a stroll around the town square. "The real question is, how do you feel about her?"

I thought about that. "I don't know," I said.

"Do better."

"Well, when she's nearby, I feel all warm and a little bit sweaty. And happy. Like maybe something really amazing is about to happen at any second."

"Go on."

"And when we're... together... you know..." I could not talk about sex with my aunt.

"I do know. I'm not dead," she said.

"Yeah, well. It's the best thing I've ever felt. And not just... like that. It's like, when I'm holding her, everything I need in the world is already right there, in my arms."

"Yup."

"But that's insane, right? We literally just met."

"Love follows its own rules, Rock."

"Love?" Shock flittered through me like ice shards flying after a hockey stop.

"It happens, honey. Even to big strong hockey players called Rock."

"Shit."

"And it seems to me like you'd better do something about it pretty fast, since you're leaving in a couple days, and right now, Drea is planning to spend those days apart."

"More shit."

"Need help?" My aunt turned to me and blinked up at me with a smile. "The drunken psychic recently confirmed that I am destined to bring the lovelorn together."

I rubbed a hand through my hair. "What?"

"The inn. That's what I'm doing. Building an inn for the lovelorn so I can matchmake."

That was a little bit of crazy I was not going to touch with a ten-foot hockey stick. But the help? I could use that. "Yeah, I have no idea what to do."

"I have a few thoughts. Come with me." Aunt Nattie took my arm and dragged me toward a shop on the other side of the square called Floral Explosion.

"It might take more than flowers, Aunt Nattie."

"Come on, Rock. Trust me."

I sighed and followed my aunt into the store, which did indeed look as if there'd been a floral explosion inside.

I did not enjoy the night I spent alone, and it seemed like such a waste, considering Drea was nearby at her friend's house, apparently miserable. Paige had called earlier, thanks to my aunt's influence, and now it felt like the entire town was somehow involved in my effort to let Drea know I was sorry. And that I wanted something real with her.

The next morning, however, my stomach was in giddy knots, and I could barely lace up my pickleball sneakers, with all the nerves firing through me.

"You okay over there, man?" Callan Whitewood, former forward for a pro soccer team in DC, was grinning at me, while a couple of his pals looked on from the opposite bench in our locker room. The soccer players were surprisingly big, especially Trace Johnson, who played keeper for the South Bay Sharks. His buddy Hamish, who had arrived to play pickleball in a kilt, was also enormous.

"You guys ever think about switching to a real sport?" I asked them, earning me a growl from Hamish.

"They're on your team, man," Callan reminded me. "Save it for the Singletree Soup Slingers."

Before long, the announcer was doing his thing, and it sounded like the court seating was pretty packed.

"Ready?" I asked the guys, who all hooted and hollered

as they picked up their paddles. The tournament would consist of two doubles matches going at the same time, with seven total matches in the first round.

We headed out to the stadium, where the other team was already prancing around for the crowd, taking bows and waving their arms in the air. They were a motley assortment of players, many of them clearly in their seventies. One lady had to be at least eighty, though she looked pretty spry in her matching track suit and neon headband.

I scanned the crowd as they cheered for my team's entrance, and immediately saw—or felt—Drea looking on. When I found her there, our eyes met briefly, though she quickly looked away.

This was going to be rough.

"Welcome to our all-star players," the announcer called, quieting the crowd. "We've got an assortment of sports stars from teams across the country. Let's hear a hearty welcome for Trace Johnson, Hamish 'The Hammer' MacEvoy, and Fernando 'the Fire' Fuerte from the South Bay Sharks!"

The crowd roared.

"And a hearty greeting for Avalanche Peters from the Smith Valley Sledders!" I'd met Peters on the ice a few times, and couldn't help the adrenaline that spiked when I heard his name. Of course, now we were on the same team. I just hoped the shit-talking would be aimed at the other team in this situation—he was famous for it.

"Finally, let's have a cheer for the Wilcox Wombats star center, Rock Stevens!"

The crowd didn't exactly go wild, but they were loud

enough to make me feel welcome. Of course, the only person I cared about being happy to see me didn't look that way at all. Drea watched me trot out onto the court with a strange look on her face. The look you might use before you disemboweled a favorite pet, if that was a face people made. Yikes.

"Before we get started with the tournament today, folks, we have a special treat for you!"

The stadium quieted as my nerves ramped up to eleven.

I held my breath as Lottie appeared with a team of women I recognized from around town—her daughters, I guessed—and they rolled out the little makeshift stage, speakers, and the enormous floral displays Lottie had commissioned, insisting that no matter what the gesture, flowers were required.

And then the music started, and the announcer shoved a microphone into my hand.

"Drea," I said into the thing as a loud squeal rent the air, earning a groan from the crowd. "Drea Coppersmith, this is for you. I thought hard about what I needed to say to you. Because there are so many things I want to say," I took a deep breath. "But when I'm lost for words, I often find that the best place to look is Broadway." I took the stage in a leap.

I heard a few sounds of surprise around me, but caught my Aunt Nattie's eye in the crowd where she and Noah sat with two of his brothers, and they all nodded. They knew. After all, my Broadway affliction was completely Aunt Nattie's fault.

The music swelled, and I began to sing "On the Street Where You Live," which Lottie and I had agreed, with my aunt's help, would be most fitting. It was about seeing regular things very differently once someone you've fallen in love with comes into your life.

I watched Drea's face as I sang to her about wanting to be nowhere more than on the street where she lives. When tears dripped down her cheeks and she turned to bury her face in Paige's shoulder, I thought I'd screwed it all up, but Paige motioned for me to come closer.

I kept singing, rather badly, I'll admit, as I climbed down from the stage and moved up into the stadium to where Drea sat. Soon, I was at the end of her aisle, and the other people seated there rose and moved away so I could approach. I finished the song standing next to her, and dropped down into a kneel as the crowd around us went completely nuts.

At least they had liked it.

"Drea," I whispered, and the crowd quieted again. "Drea, babe. I'm sorry. It's killing me that you think I used you or manipulated you... It wasn't my intention. The thing is, I think I realized, even when you were poking me with your very pointy finger that first night, that there was something here, something worth exploring."

She was looking at me now, her little pout right there, begging me to kiss it off her face, but I held back.

"I have loved every minute I've spent with you this week," I told her. "And I can't stop myself from imagining lots more minutes. And maybe whole days. Or even... years."

"We just met," she whispered, but her eyes gleamed.

"We did," I agreed. "But this week really has changed everything for me. The song was the best explanation of how I feel. It's like I see the everything differently just knowing you're alive."

"Rock," she whispered, half giggling, half crying.

"Speak up!" Someone in the crowd yelled, and I realized then that the microphone was still on. I thought about making a gesture, but this wasn't hockey. It was pickleball. And I was trying to win the heart of the woman I was falling in love with.

"I'm not asking for forever. Not yet at least," I told her, taking her soft delicate hand. "But I'm asking for a chance. Can you give me that?"

Drea stood, pulling me to my feet in the process, and she stepped close, putting her arms around me and tilting her chin up to look into my eyes.

"I can give you that," she said, and then she rose up onto her toes to kiss me hard. "But only if you promise never to sing again."

"That bad?" I said, partially offended.

"It wasn't good," she told me. "But, actually, I loved it."

"Good, because Broadway is in my blood."

"Wonderful."

"You got the girl," Avalanche called from the court. "Can we play some pickleball now?"

"Let's rumble!" The old woman in the track suit shrieked.

And for the rest of the day, I played the best—and only —pickleball I'd ever played, knowing the woman I loved was cheering me on, and that later, we'd go home. Together.

I didn't know what the future would bring, but I was pretty sure Drea Coppersmith would be a big part of it.

THE END

EPILOGUE - JULIUS RAMON (ZAMBONI DRIVER)

ANOTHER MATCH.

And my heart is happy.

I spend a lot of time with this team. But they don't see me as one of their own, not really. I drive the Zamboni, I sweep the ice. And I stand in the shadows, silently living a whole new life through these men.

Because when they skate, I don't see them.

I see my own shadow. The man I once was.

And though I love the game, and I hold these boys close to me, looking after them like sons, there is one thing about the Wilcox Wombats I cannot abide: Almost all of them are still alone, putting the game over all else and calling it happiness.

I know better than most… nothing rivals the satisfaction found in loving another person completely.

I had that chance, and I let it go.

And while I might not have much control over anything beyond the Zamboni when it comes to the Wombats, I have a bit. And I'll use it if I have to in order to make sure none of them make the same mistake I did.

Want more Wombats? Grab the first full-length book in the Wilcox Wombats series here!

Turn the page for a sneak peek!

1. THE WEDDING WINGER SNEAK PEEK

CHAPTER ONE - SLY REMINGTON

"Hey, hey, there. Not without a coaster, man." Stephano Mizzoni lifted my beer and slid a little round cork puck beneath it on the bar top.

"Sorry, Mom," I quipped, catching Rock's eye and sharing a laugh.

"Don't you have any doilies you could put down, Mizzoni? I think my butt's sweating onto your barstool here," Rock added.

Mizzoni didn't crack a smile. Instead he stepped between us, looking at us with murder in his gaze. "When you are the first in your family to own more than a shoebox, you come talk to me about how you want to take care of your things," he says, his voice low and threatening.

I clapped him on the back and picked up my beer. "No big deal man, and the place is incredible. I don't blame you for wanting to keep it pristine."

He nodded, his shoulders loosening visibly.

Rock was still chuckling, but I shot him a hard look and he zipped it.

Mizzoni had just bought the place, and I had to admit, it was pretty insane. Two floors of glass overlooked a backyard pool, grounds that most national parks would envy, and an outdoor kitchen and bar nicer than most people had inside their homes. The bar was wood, but it had a glossy finish that suggested it wasn't going to be marred by one cold beer can—especially since it was built to be outside here in Virginia, where the weather was far from perfect most of the time—but it was his call to keep us in line. And while every one of these guys got out of line now and then, it wouldn't happen at a teammate's new house.

I sauntered across the yard, enjoying the steamy heat of the early June evening and the knowledge that we had a couple months to enjoy before we retook the ice together as the Wilcox Wombats.

If you're thinking it's an unusual name for an American pro hockey team, you're not wrong. But also, shut it. The name is distinctive, and getting on the wrong side of a whole hockey team isn't advisable.

"Sly," Chris Houstein called from one of the loungers poolside. "Where's this month's flavor?" Chris was a second-string winger, and while I loved the guy like I loved all the guys I played with, he had a big mouth.

He was sitting with Deck Gillespie and Tyler "Corny" Cornwall, soaking up the last rays of the day, margaritas in hand. I took the lounger to one side of the little group and kicked back.

"Didn't think I needed the distraction tonight. Wanted to enjoy celebrating the season with you guys."

"Rock didn't get the memo," Deck said, his eyes back on the bar where Rock Stevens, our center, sat on a barstool with his fiancee Drea standing between his legs. His hand was on her ass, and the way they were making out told me they were probably minutes from slipping inside for a few minutes. I wondered if Mizzoni had a bunch of rules about hockey players fucking on his furniture too. Probably. But it wasn't my problem.

"Remember, fiancees are different than puck bunnies," Corny said.

"I don't date puck bunnies," I said, but there was no steam in my words. I only dated puck bunnies and other women who were interested in the lifestyle, the prominence that being seen with me brought them. There was no danger of...well, anything, really, if the understanding between us was clear from the start.

"RIght," Deck said, slurping his margarita noisily and then eyeballing it. "These are ridiculous. I don't think Mizzoni followed the recipe when he loaded that machine he bought."

We all glanced back at the bar, where Freddy Elks and Cade Simpson were pouring another bottle of tequila into the top of the machine. "He had help," I noted.

I leaned back, letting my eyes slip shut and the sound of the music and my teammates' banter float around me. This was perfect. This was everything I needed in life. Almost.

We'd hang out here all night. Half the guys would sleep where they fell, and in the morning we'd strategize when to do it again. We'd be back at practice soon enough, but for now, we got to be just friends. A family, really. And it was one of the best feelings in the world.

Which was why it kind of sucked that I couldn't stay long, but I wasn't making my exit quite yet. I needed a few hours of this before I headed back home to face the work waiting for me there.

"You guys want to go to Europe this summer?" Deck asked.

I opened my eyes and sat up a bit. "What's your plan?"

"Thinking about renting a house or something. Someplace nice."

"Italy," Freddy suggested. "Then we get to call it a villa."

Corny sighed and didn't bother opening his eyes to say, "The Amalfi coast. But it's likely to be crowded this year since the pandemic's officially over and everything. Prices will probably go back up. I can ask my dad about the boat." Corny grew up wealthy. But not just drive-a-nice-car and have someone else clean your floors rich. His family owned islands and vineyards and probably a few small countries. Most of the time you wouldn't have known it, though.

"Shit, could you see us floating around the Mediterranean?" Deck laughed.

"Definitely," I said, wondering what the wifi would be like. Could I pull that off and still keep up my courseload? Could I figure how to get a month off? My phone buzzed in my pocket, interrupting my thoughts. I slid it out, happy to see Beck's name pop up. I hadn't talked to my brother in a while, and I was pretty sure he was calling to congratulate us on a good season.

"Little brother, what's good?" I asked, a crazy sense of fulfillment washing through me. Life was pretty fucking perfect.

"I've got news, Sly." Beck sounded happy, so no alarms blared within me. We were a little worried about Dad's health, and the potential for bad news was always in the back of my mind, but it didn't sound like this was that call.

"What's going on?"

"I'm engaged, man. Zara and I are getting married."

I sat up, raising my beer to my brother, though he couldn't see it. "Congratulations, man!" I pulled the phone away from my ear and shouted, "My little brother's getting married!"

The guys all cheered and lifted drinks to toast my brother. Some of them had met Beckett, most of them hadn't. It didn't matter — this was how it was. We had each other's backs in everything. Celebrated together, mourned together.

"That's awesome," I told him. "When's the wedding?"

"Soon, actually. That's why I'm calling. Beginning of August. Think you can make it?"

I didn't even have to think about it. "Of course."

"Will you be my best man?"

"Definitely. I'm honored, little bro."

"There's, uh… there's just one thing." Beck said.

"What's that?"

"Mom says you can't bring one of your usual dates."

I hadn't even thought about that yet, but now I felt irritated. "Why not? What if I'm in love too?"

"Are you?"

"Of course not."

"So… maybe just come on your own? Unless you're really dating someone." Beck sounded hesitant, unhappy to be delivering that specific message.

"Don't worry about that, bro. You just enjoy this part of your life. I'll be there, I'll bring someone appropriate--wait, what are the bridesmaids like?"

"No."

"What do you mean, 'no'?"

"Zara's friends won't meet your requirements, anyway."

"You have no idea what my requirements are," I said, working to sound indignant.

"Let's see… focused on your fame, usually augmented with silicone, generally challenged when it comes to procuring clothing in appropriate sizes—"

"That's enough." I growled it, not because any of it was wrong, but because it didn't need my dating habits to be examined too closely.

"I'm sending the info via email," Beck told me. "See you soon!"

"Can't wait." I hung up, but almost as soon as I ended the call, the phone was buzzing again. Mom.

I stood and walked away from the peanut gallery next to the pool. "Hi Mom."

"Sylvestor, honey. Great season. I'm so proud of you. Your father is over the moon."

"Thanks, Mom." It still warmed my insides to hear Mom say she was proud of me.

"Did you speak with your brother?"

"He just called."

"Isn't it wonderful? I just love Zara."

"She's great. I'm really happy for them." I was. I'd always pictured my little brother with the standard two kids and a dog, and he was on his way down that path now. It was good. Mom needed some grandkids, and they sure as hell weren't coming from me.

"And he told you the other thing?"

My good mood dampened. "I'm not bringing a date, if that's what you mean. I've been advised."

"Honey," she said, giving me her 'be reasonable' tone. "It isn't that we don't like your little girlfriends—"

"I'll just come on my own, Mom." I interrupted her before she could give me another description of my recent lady friends.

"I just…" Mom trailed off, and I thought I heard her sniff. "I just wish you'd work a little harder on finding the right kind of woman. Someone real. Someone who you can—"

"It's fine, Mom."

"I hate you being alone."

I laughed, and the words were out before I could really think about them. "I'm rarely alone."

"Ew."

"Sorry."

"Anyway, that's why I'm calling." She hesitated. "I have someone I want you to meet."

Alarm bells rang loud and clear in my head. "No thanks. I'm good."

"We'll see."

"Mom." I made my voice stern and low. "No setups." The last thing I needed was to break the heart of a daughter of Mom's friends or colleagues. Better to keep my dating habits far, far away from family.

"The engagement party is next week. I'll have your room ready. Come on Thursday. Party's on Saturday night at Pete's." Pete was Zara's dad, who we'd known for years. He lived on the other side of town, and his house was ideal for big parties. He wasn't Corny wealthy, but he did just fine.

"Okay. I'll come home Thursday."

"Can't wait to see you."

"Love you." I hung up and glanced around the yard. The barbecue was fired up, my teammates were happy and relaxed. And my enthusiasm for hanging out had been zapped. I didn't like to sneak out, but I knew they wouldn't let me go, so I slipped out the side gate, hopped into my car, and headed home to study.

2. THE WEDDING WINGER SNEAK PEEK

CHAPTER TWO - CLARA CONNOR

"This day has gone to shit."

"Tell me about it," my best friend Andie laughed on the other end of the phone.

"No. Seriously. I'm covered in bear shit."

"You are the only person who can say that, you know. I mean, the only person who can say it and actually mean that you are literally covered in shit."

"Well, that's something, I guess. I do mean it somewhat figuratively too." I was almost back to my truck, which was the only reason I had any service at all. It had been a brutally long day in the field, and I was hot, and sticky. And covered in… well, you got it.

"Hey, what are you up to tonight?" Andie had this way of asking about my plans with a lilt in her voice that made it sound like she had something absolutely incredible up her sleeve, like if I only said yes, my whole life would change.

"Showering. Picking up Katie. Probably not in that order, though."

"What if…" she drew this out, and I knew she thought she was going to have to convince me about whatever it was. I unlocked the truck and slid in behind the wheel, starting it up and doing my best to sync Andie's pause with the natural pause caused by the phone switching to the car speaker. "What do you think?"

"Sorry. Missed that." As I pulled the truck out onto the highway, my exhaustion sank in. We'd been tracking a couple momma bears for a few days, and had finally gotten one of them collared late this afternoon. The rest of the crew had been just steps ahead of me pulling out and heading home. I needed some sleep.

"I said, what do you think about hitting the new club downtown? I got us on the VIP list."

Oh god. That sounded legitimately awful. The groan I let out must've given away my complete lack of desire to shove myself into some tight pants and then suffer through inappropriate come-on lines all night while doing my best to drink enough to handle the overwhelming anxiety of a club while not drinking so much that I'd collapse from sheer exhaustion. Plus, there was Katie.

"Andie, I can't tonight. I'm like the walking dead. I need sleep."

I could practically hear the pout on the other end of the phone. "But you're my wingwoman and I need to get laid."

"Don't we all?" I laughed. Andie and I had been best friends since high school, and while I'd taken a short detour into the land of totally ill-advised marriages and had a baby before I could gracefully handle a shot of tequila, Andie had remained single. And she was really good at tequila.

"So, here's our chance!"

"Honestly," I told her as I navigated the highway offramp and headed toward home, "if the opportunity arose tonight, I'd probably sleep through it. Besides, I'm kind of tired of random hookups. There are no decent guys around Half Full. We've met them all."

"That's why a new club might mean fresh meat!"

"Hon…"

"I know. I can hear in your voice how tired you are. Maybe tomorrow?"

I thought about it. "I don't think I can ask Mrs. Remington for another night. Plus, the whole strategy behind raising reasonable humans is actually spending some time with them, I think. Katie already throws a fit every time I take her next door."

"Yeah," Andie said, finally giving in. "Katie deserves some mom time."

"You could come hang out with us?"

"Tomorrow? Pizza and Auntie Andie night?"

"If you want. But we'll understand if you'd rather get laid. It's Saturday night."

She sighed. "Nah, I'll come hang out with you guys. You're more fun."

"Maybe you're doing it wrong then. I'll draw you a picture when you come over tomorrow."

"Funny."

I pulled into my driveway, ignoring the slightly stagnant feeling that always came over me as I did, like a form of deja vu that didn't get realized since I'd never actually left. I'd lived in this house my entire life, with the exception of the four years I was away for school and the two years my rapidly fizzling marriage had lasted. But my parents were gone, so now it was mine.

"Night, friend," I told Andie, idling in the driveway, switching off the light.

"Night. Love you."

"Same."

I switched off the truck, ending the call, and then did a quick sniff check. Pretty bad, but Mrs. Remington had definitely seen me at my worst, considering she'd lived next door my whole life. She'd witnessed my serious acne phase, the poorly planned perm phase, and also that phase we do not discuss. The one where I was in love with her son and made a complete fool of myself on the daily through two full years of high school.

But those days were over. We'd all moved on, and now she was the cheapest and most capable babysitter I had. And I needed to thank her, get Katie, and get us both to bed.

I locked the truck and headed to the doorstep next door, stamping my feet on the lawn as I went, in hopes of getting most of the forest debris and muck off before I tracked it up her steps.

"There you are," Mrs. Remington cried, pulling the door open before I could knock.

"I'm so sorry to be late. Again."

"Oh, honey, you know I don't mind at all. You and Katie

just make my days! Heaven knows Sam isn't much fun these days."

I could hear the television blaring from the front room where Mr. Remington liked to watch whatever sports were on, with little regard for team loyalty or preference. Unless it was hockey, of course. Then he only rooted for the Wombats. For good reason.

"Well, I sure appreciate your help. I wish there was some way I could repay you. I honestly don't know what I'd do without you." It was the same conversation we had almost every time I picked Katie up. Only tonight, Mrs. Remington had a strange look on her face, a kind of half smile twinned with a little upturn of her rosy lips on one said. She looked uncertain, and devious.

"Actually, Clara… there is a little something I was hoping you'd be willing to do."

I was exhausted, but I owed this woman. So. Much. "Sure," I said, coaxing some energy into my voice. "What is it?"

"Just a little favor of your time is all."

"I'm happy to help," I told her.

She clapped her hands just as Katie appeared next to her, poking her blond head out to the side of Mrs. Remington's legs. "Hi Mommy."

"Hey Katie-bear. How was your night?"

"Good," Katie smiled. "We made krispy treats."

"Fun," I said, reaching for the little girl who made the sun and moon rise and fall in my world. She moved into my arms and I hoisted her onto my hip.

"You smell poopy."

I buried my nose in her hair for a few breaths and let out a laugh that was more of a sigh. "I know. Sorry, baby."

"No, it's okay. You smell like you."

And there it was. I was the mommy who usually smelled like bear shit. This was my life.

"We should get going to bed. And to shower," I told Mrs. Remington.

"So we'll see you Thursday night?"

"Thursday? Sorry?"

"You said you wanted to repay me."

"Oh, right." I was happy to help her out with whatever. She probably needed some help moving the boxes she'd been mentioning in the attic. "Happy to help. What time?"

"Six o'clock should be good." She smiled, and I caught another glimpse of that look, but was too tired to consider it. "Dress up a little. We'll have dinner."

Oh. Dinner. Maybe she was just lonely, seeing as how Sam never moved out of his chair by the TV anymore. "Um, sure. See you then," I told her, turning with my arms full of little girl.

She watched us head to our house and stood on the doorstep until we were safely inside. That was the kind of people the Remingtons were. Most of them, at least.

Want the rest? Grab it here.

Want to make sure you never miss a new Wombats release? Sign up for Delancey's Fancy here (her newsletter).

ALSO BY DELANCEY STEWART

Want more? Get early releases, sneak peeks and freebies! Join my mailing list at www.delanceystewart.com or scan the QR code and get a free story!

The WILCOX WOMBATS Series:

Checking the Center

The Wedding Winger

Grumpy Goalie

Puck Proposal

The KASPER RIDGE Series:

Only a Summer

Only a Fling

Only a Crush

Only a Secret

Only a Touch

Only a Chance

The SINGLETREE Series:

Happily Ever His

Happily Ever Hers

Shaking the Sleigh

Second Chance Spring

Falling Into Forever

The DIGITAL DATING Series (with Marika Ray):

Texting with the Enemy

While You Were Texting

Save the Last Text

How to Lose a Girl in 10 Texts

The Text Before Christmas

The MR. MATCH Series:

Prequel: Scoring a Soulmate

Book One: Scoring the Keeper's Sister

Book Two: Scoring a Fake Fiancée

Book Three: Scoring a Prince

Book Four: Scoring with the Boss

Book Five: Scoring a Holiday Match

Mr. Match: The Boxed Set

*The **KINGS GROVE** Series:*

When We Let Go

Open Your Eyes

When We Fall

Open Your Heart

Christmas in Kings Grove

*The **STARR RANCH WINERY** Series:*

Chasing a Starr

***THE GIRLFRIENDS OF GOTHAM** Series:*

Men and Martinis

Highballs in the Hamptons

Cosmos and Commitment

STANDALONES:

Let it Snow

Without Words

Without Promises